This Book Belongs To:

This is a Parragon Book
This edition published in 2007

Parragon
Queen Street House,
4 Queen Street, BATH BA1 1HE, UK

This book was created by small world creations ltd

Printed in China

ISBN 978-1-4054-1595-8

Fred the Fearless Fireman

p

Fred Fireman hurried to the fire station. It was his turn to cook lunch for the firemen on his shift, and he had just bought some nice, plump sausages at the butcher's.

At the fire station, Fred bumped into Builder Benny, who had come to repair a broken window frame.

"Ooops! Hello, Benny!" he said.

Then he went straight to the kitchen to start cooking.

The smell of sausages wafted through the fire station.

"Mmm, those sausages smell good!" said Dan and Mike,
the other firemen, as they arrived for work.

Suddenly the alarm bell rang –

CLANG! CLANG! CLANG!

"Emergency!" cried Fireman Mike. He and Fireman Dan rushed down the pole and into their fire-fighting gear.

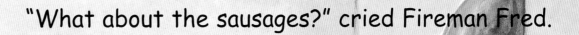

"What about the sausages?" cried Fireman Fred.

"Don't worry about a thing," said Builder Benny, coming in through the window. "I'll look after them till you get back."

"Thanks, Benny!" said Fireman Fred, trying to get his apron off as he rushed down to join the others.

The emergency
was in Tony's Pizza Parlour
- one of the ovens had caught fire!
"We'll have that blaze out in a jiffy!" said Fred, rushing in
with a big fire extinguisher. Dan and Mike followed with the hose.

With a WHISH! and a WHOOSH! from Fred,
and a SPLISH! and a SPLOOSH! from Mike and Dan,
the fire was soon out.

Just when they were ready to go back to the station, the firemen heard a call coming through over their radio.

"Emergency! Emergency! Window cleaner in distress on Pine Avenue. Emergency! Over."

"We're on our way!" said Fireman Fred, starting the engine. "Over and out!"

NEE-NAW! NEE-NAW!

With sirens blaring, the fire engine zoomed into Pine Avenue. A crowd had gathered around Tip-Top Towers, the tallest building in town.

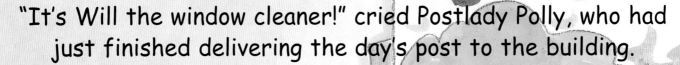

"It's Will the window cleaner!" cried Postlady Polly, who had just finished delivering the day's post to the building.

"His ladder has broken, and he's hurt his leg. Now he's stuc and he can't get down! Can you help him?"

"Certainly!" said Fireman Fred. "I'll be up there in a jiffy!"

The firemen put up
their tallest ladder.
While Mike and Dan
held out a net - just in
case - Fred fearlessly
began scrambling up
the ladder.

"Here I come, Will!"
he shouted.

"I've got you, Will!" said Fred, grabbing hold of the window cleaner. As the crowd below cheered, Fred Carried Will down the ladder and helped him into the fire engine.

Fred drove the fire engine straight to the hospital.
"Thank you for rescuing me," Will said to Fred.

"Don't mention it," said Fred. "I'm sure your leg will be fine -
but I think you'll need a new ladder!"

"What a busy day it's been!"
said Fireman Fred, as they drove
back to the fire station.
"I feel really frazzled!"

Fire Station

"Our work's not over yet!" said Fireman Dan.
"Look! There's smoke up ahead!

NEE-NAW! NEE-NAW! went the siren.

VRROOOM! VRROOOM! went the engine,
as it raced to the scene of the fire.

The smoke was coming from the fire
station! Dan and Mike unwound the hose,
and Fred raced inside. "Oof!" he gasped, as he
tripped over the hose and bumped into Benny - again!

"Sorry, fellows," said a red-faced Builder Benny.
"I guess I burnt the sausages. I think your lunch is ruined."

Poor Fred felt really frazzled now - until he had an idea.

"Tony!" said Fireman Fred.
"His pizzas are yummy, and an extra-large one
will be a perfect lunch for all of us!"